Sarah 'n' Dippity

Written by Gerald R. Stanek

Illustrated by Joyce Huntington Stanek

ITHACA, NEW YORK

Shiver Hill Books
18 Sunset West Circle
Ithaca, NY 14850
shiver@twcny.rr.com

Library of Congress Control Number: 2003098376

ISBN 0-9747417-0-1

There is a girl named Sarah I know.
She has reddish hair, and hazel eyes, and freckles.

She has a mom and a dad,
and a hamster named Elgin,
and a cat named Buster.

Buster has reddish hair, and hazel eyes, and whiskers, and a tail.

Elgin has reddish hair, and whitish hair, and teeny tiny eyes, and sometimes Sarah can't tell which end is his head and which is his tail.

Elgin isn't allowed
out of his cage...

and Buster isn't allowed out of the house.

Sarah also has a friend named Dippity.
Dippity has reddish hair, hazel eyes,
and freckles, and wings.

Dippity doesn't like to talk, so some people don't notice her. Sarah says that's okay, because she's bashful too.

Dippity doesn't play much, but she's great to have around, because she can go anywhere and see everything. Dippity is always helping Sarah find things, but they aren't always the things Sarah is looking for.

Most of the time, what Sarah is looking for is Buster, because they play hide and seek a lot. Of course, it's usually Buster that does the hiding.

One time, when Sarah was calling out 'Buuuuussterrr!', she saw Dippity, who was pointing at the couch.

So Sarah went and looked under the pillows and the cushions, but Buster wasn't there.

Still, Dippity pointed at the couch, so Sarah got down on the floor and looked under the couch.

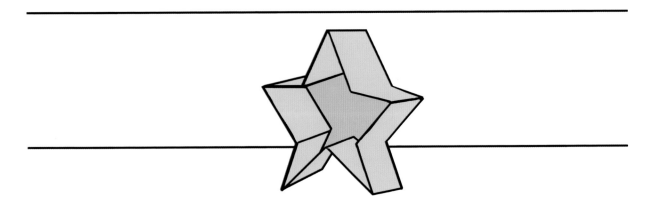

Buster wasn't *there* either, but waaayyy in the back, by the wall, was......the star shape!

"Oh!" Sarah exclaimed, and she took it and ran to show it to her mother.

"Oh! The star!" Sarah's mother said, "It's been missing for soooo long, hasn't it!"

"Yeah," agreed Sarah, "It's been missing for hours.... and days, and... and... hundreds of times."

"Yes, it has," Sarah's mother said. "Where did you find it?"

"Dippity found it," Sarah said.

"Oh, he did, did he?" Sarah's mom is one of those people who never notice Dippity, even when she's right in front of them.

"She, Mommy. I told you before, Dippity's a girl."

"Right, she. Well it's good that you and Dippity found that. Now we can put it with the others."

"Yeah," Sarah said, and they went and found the toy with all the shapes, and fit the star in.

Once, when Sarah's Mom was doing dishes (but really talking on the phone), and Sarah was eating lunch (but really watching T.V. upside down); Dippity began flying around in a circle and pointing excitedly.

"What is it, Dippity? What's the matter?" Sarah asked. As usual, Dippity said nothing.

Sarah looked where she was pointing, and that was how she discovered that Buster liked tuna fish.

That was a good thing to know, because Sarah doesn't like tuna fish. Dippity is always helping out that way.

Another time, when Sarah was calling 'Buuuuussterrr!', she followed Dippity into the kitchen.

Dippity was pointing to the counter top, so Sarah climbed up to look.

Buster wasn't there, but there *was* a plate of cookies!

"Thanks, Dippity!" Sarah said. She took two of the cookies and sat down on the chair to eat them.

They were very yummy, but when her mother saw her, she was upset.

"Sarah Eliza McStew!" she yelled, "What do you think you're doing?"

"They're cookies, Mommy," Sarah explained, "Do you want one? They're really, really, good. Dippity found them, and she showed me where they were!"

"Oh, so it's all Dippity's doing, is it? Well, all I can say is, that Dippity had better ask permission next time, before helping herself to cookies. Do you understand, me, young lady?"

"Yes," Sarah said, "But Dippity didn't have any Mommy; she never eats anything."

One day, when Sarah was looking for something to do, and was just thinking about calling 'Buuuuusterrr!', Dippity came fluttering by, motioning Sarah to follow her, so she did.

Dippity led Sarah right to Buster, before she had even called 'Buuuuussterrr!', or asked Dippity for help, or anything!

But Buster seemed kind of funny. He wasn't curled up sleeping,

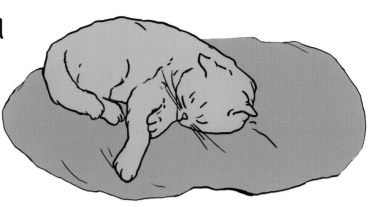

and he wasn't taking a bath,

and he wasn't stretching or hissing

or meowing or eating.

He was just lying on top of the washing machine, with his paws over the edge and his ears straight up, and his big hazel eyes staring at the floor!

The only part of him moving was his tail, which slowwllly twitched back and forth.

The strangest thing was, he wasn't running away from Sarah! That was how Sarah knew something was wrong. She ran to tell her mom.

"Mommy!" she began, but her mom wanted to talk first. "Sarah, did you unlock Elgin's cage?" her mother asked.

"No. Mommy, come quick!" Sarah said, but her mother was busy rearranging the living room furniture. "Mommy can't come right now honey, Elgin is missing, and we have to find him."

"Oh no!" Sarah cried. "Elgin's missing and Buster's sick!"

"What?" her mother asked. "What do you mean Buster's sick?"

"He won't play hide and seek with me, Mommy," Sarah explained, "Come see!" she begged, pulling her mother into the laundry room.

"See? He won't move or run or meow or anything!" Sarah said, almost in tears.

Sarah's mom was smiling.

"Good job, Buster!" she said, "He's not sick, Sarah, he's found Elgin!"

"He has?"

"Yes!" Sarah's mother replied, as she got down on the floor. "See?"

Sarah got down on the floor too, and peered
between the washing machine and the dryer.

It was all black there, except for two teeny tiny shiny dots that she could tell were Elgin's eyes.

"Hey!" she yelled, "It's Elgin. What are you doing under there Elgin?" As usual, Elgin didn't say anything.

Soon Elgin was safely back in his cage...

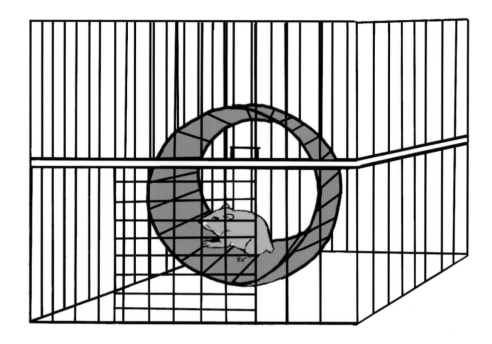

and Buster was his old self again.

"Boy, that was lucky how I was almost looking for Buster, and Dippity knew that I was almost looking for Buster and showed me where Buster was, and I knew he was sick or... gone crazy or something and I ran and got you, and Elgin just happened to be hiding there where Buster was going crazy, huh, Mommy, that was sure lucky that Dippity knew I was almost looking for Buster, huh," Sarah said.

"Well," Sarah's mother sighed, "all I know is, it's a good thing for everyone that Sarah 'n' Dippity are around.

"Yeah," agreed Sarah.

Serendipity-
an apparent aptitude for making
fortunate discoveries.